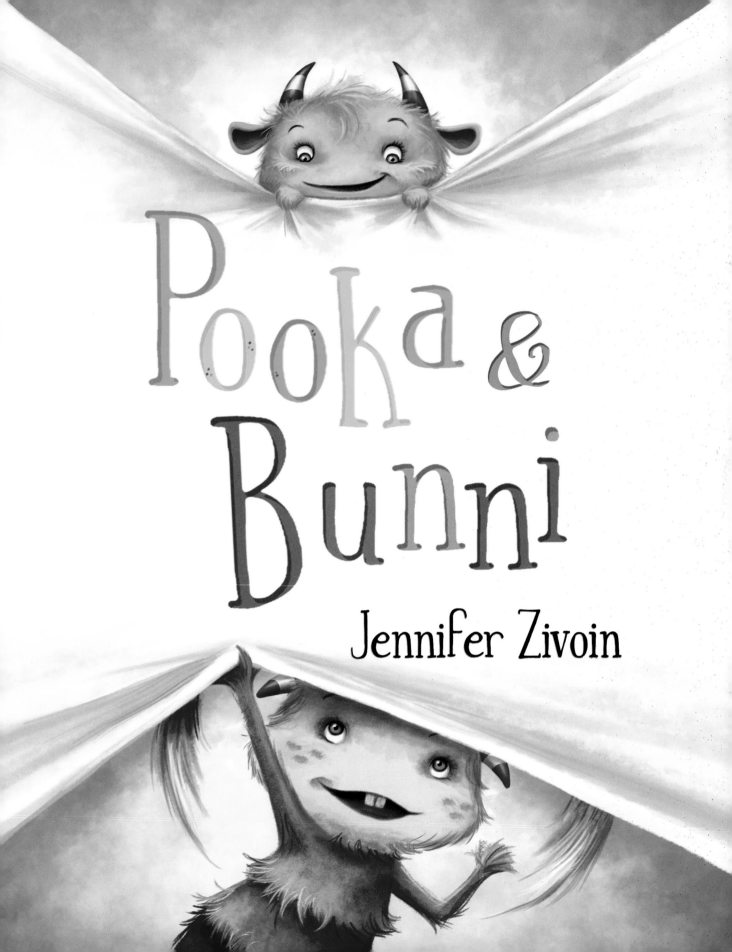

# Pooka & Bunni

## Jennifer Zivoin

With love for Olivia and Elyse.
I know you can do it.
You are big inside!–JZ

Books for Kids From the
American Psychological Association

Copyright © 2020 by Jennifer Zivoin. Published in 2020 by Magination Press, an imprint
of the American Psychological Association. All rights reserved.  Except as permitted under
the United States Copyright Act of 1976, no part of this publication may be reproduced or
distributed in any form or by any means, or stored in a database or retrieval system, without
the prior written permission of the publisher.

Magination Press is a registered trademark of the American Psychological Association.
Order books at maginationpress.org, or call 1-800-374-2721.

Book design by Rachel Ross
Printed by Phoenix Color, Hagerstown, MD

Library of Congress Cataloging-in-Publication Data
Names: Zivoin, Jennifer, author.
Title: Pooka & Bunni / written and illustrated by Jennifer Zivoin.
Other titles: Pooka and Bunni
Description: Washington, DC : Magination Press, an imprint of the American Psychological
Association, 2020. | Summary: Pooka always wants to do whatever her big sister, Bunni, is
doing but when she knocks down Bunni's pillow castle, she needs imagination, creativity, and
perseverance to set things right.

Identifiers: LCCN 2019056330 | ISBN 9781433832147 (hardcover)
Subjects: CYAC: Problem solving—Fiction. | Ability—Fiction. | Size—Fiction. | Sisters—Fiction.
Classification: LCC PZ7.1.Z6 Poo 2020 | DDC [E]—dc23
LC record available at https://lccn.loc.gov/2019056330

Manufactured in the United States of America
10 9 8 7 6 5 4 3 2 1

This is Bunni...

and this is Pooka.

Bunni is big, clever, and
interested in many things.

Pooka is small, clever, and interested in
whatever Bunni is doing.

Where are you going?

Can I watch?

Can I help?

You're too little to help!
You'll just knock everything down.

I have to go to my whistling lesson, Pooka!
Don't touch my castle while I'm gone!
It's not done yet, and it has to be perfect.

Oooh!

It's a circus!

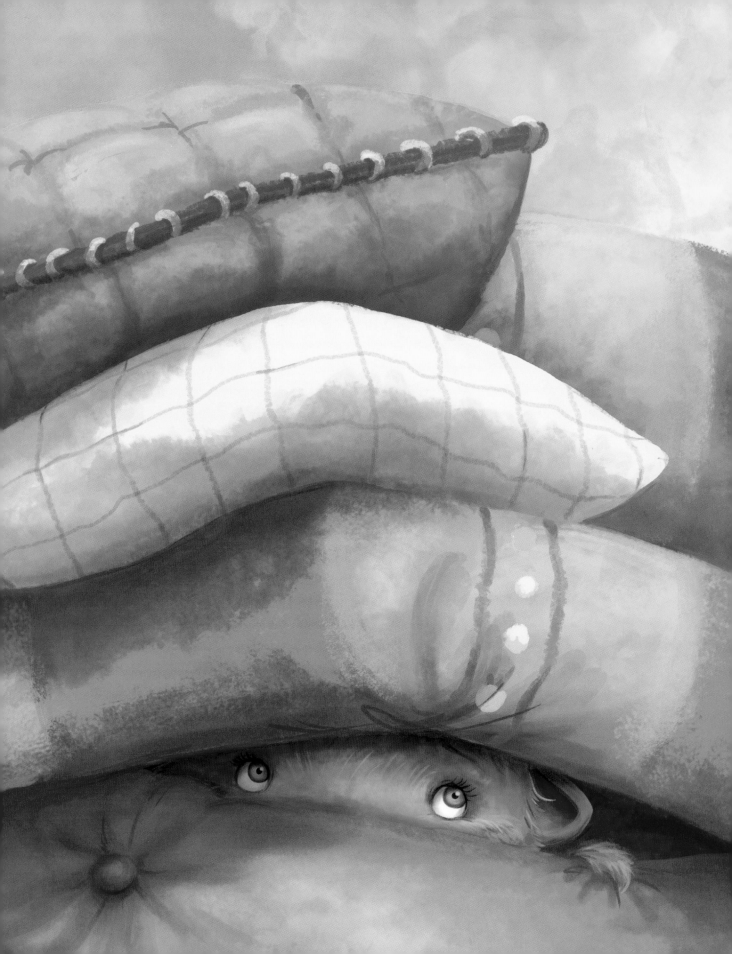

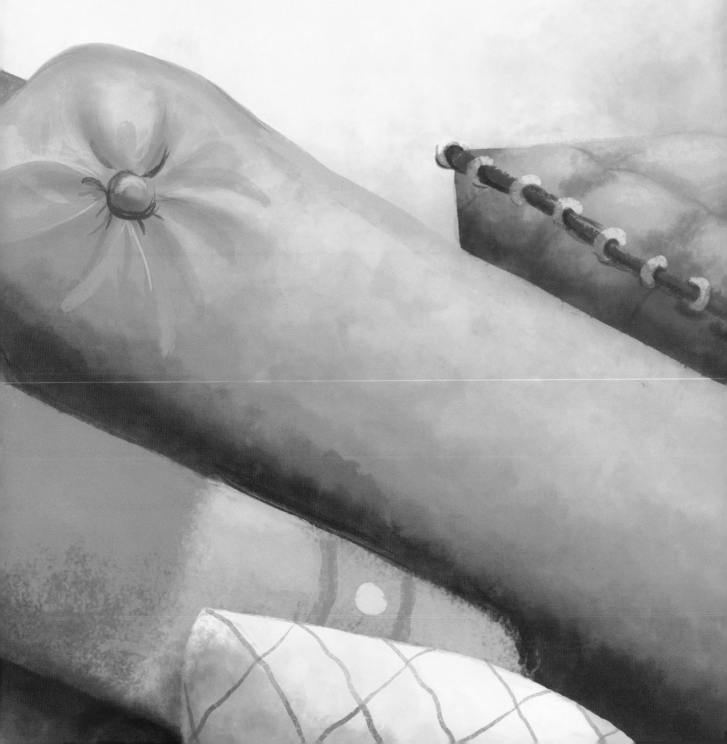

Uh oh...

Pooka gives a big push...

...stacks and climbs and lifts...

...and falls. She gave a big try, but it did not work.

Pooka gives a big yell...

... and a big kick, but that doesn't work either.

So, Pooka stops and thinks.

Bunni was right. Pooka is too
little to move big things.

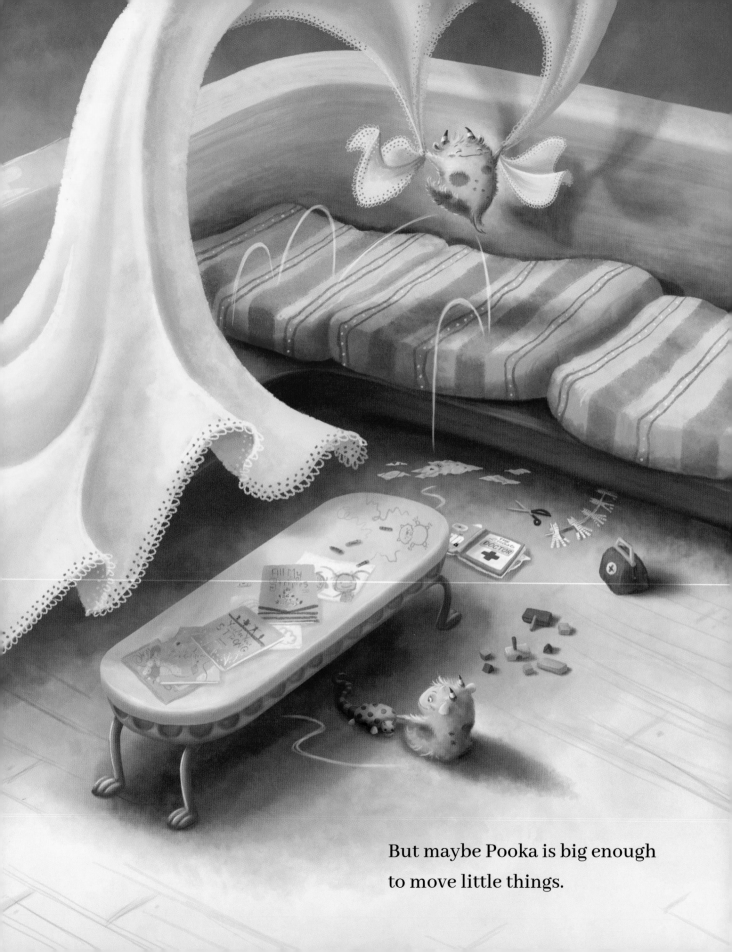

But maybe Pooka is big enough
to move little things.

I can pick up the pieces
of my messes...

...and stick them back together.

I can carry some big things
if I make them lighter...

...and some big things aren't
heavy for me at all!

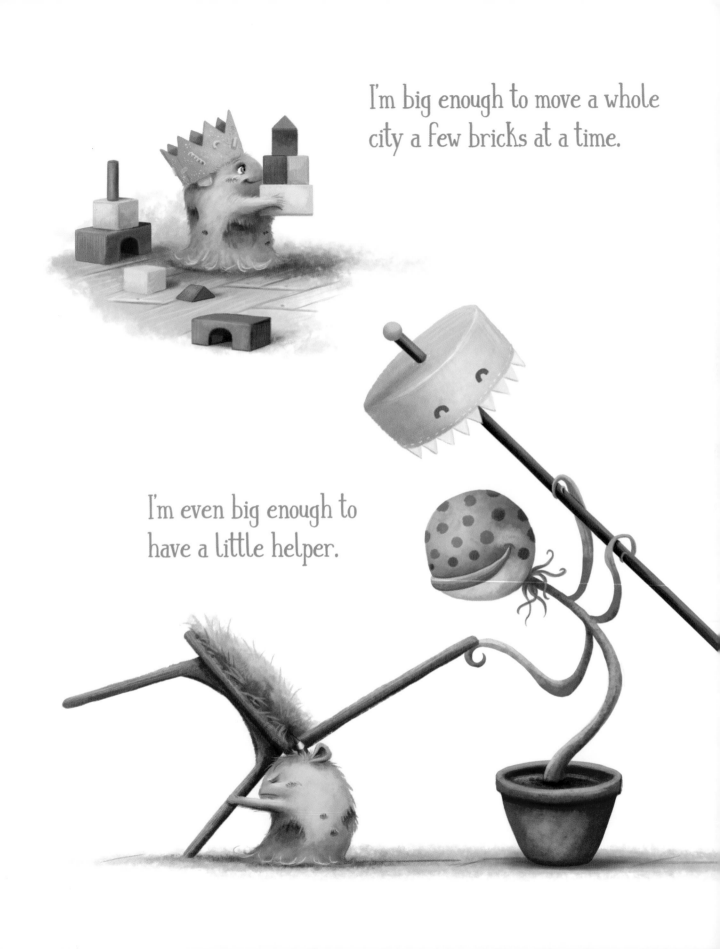

I'm big enough to move a whole city a few bricks at a time.

I'm even big enough to have a little helper.

I KNOW I can do this.
I AM big...on the INSIDE!

# POOKA!

Um...hi, Bunni!

Welcome back?

Look at what you did!

It's
perfect!

Careful, Bunni!
Don't touch!

Don't worry, Bunni. We can build
an even better castle together!